WANTED:
The Planet Hunters.

CRIME:
Galactic Terrorism.

WEAPON:
The Nethergun.

WHEREABOUTS:
Sector 90.

YOUR MISSION:
Get inside their starship and capture them!

Bantam Books in the
Be An Interplanetary Spy Series

BE AN INTERPLANETARY SPY ™ ⑩

PLANET HUNTERS

by Seth McEvoy
illustrated by Darrel Anderson

A Byron Preiss Book

BANTAM BOOKS
TORONTO • NEW YORK • LONDON • SYDNEY • AUCKLAND

To Andrea Brown

Seth McEvoy, author, is an active member of the Science Fiction Writers of America: is a video game designer and programmer; has written a biocritical study of science fiction author Samuel R. Delany for Frederick Ungar, Publishers; has also written *How to Program Arcade Games on the Timex 1500 Computer* and *How to Program Arcade Games on the T199 4a Computer* for Computer Books, and *Create-A-Game on the VIC-20* for Dell Books.

Darrel Anderson is an artist who specializes in the speculative and fantastic. His background includes drafting, architectural rendering and commercial illustration. His most recent projects include illustrations for a computer game based on Arthur C. Clarke's *Breaking Strain* and illustrations for two books in the *Be An Interplanetary Spy* series.

RL 4, IL age 9 and up

PLANET HUNTERS
A Bantam Book / May 1985

Special thanks to Alex Jay.
Cover art by Steve Fastner.
Cover design by Alex Jay.
Logo and series design by Marc Hempel.
Additional design and production by Susan Hui Leung.
Typesetting by David E. Seham Associates, Inc.

ISBN 0-553-24532-5

Published simultaneously in the United States and Canada

Printed and bound in Great Britain by Hunt Barnard Printing Ltd.

O   0 9 8 7 6 5 4 3 2 1

Introduction

You are an Interplanetary Spy. You are about to embark on a dangerous mission. On your mission you will face challenges that may result in your death.

You work for the Interplanetary Spy Center, a far-reaching organization devoted to stopping crime and terrorism in the galaxy. While you are on your mission, you will take your orders from the Interplanetary Spy Center. Follow your instructions carefully.

You will be traveling alone on your mission. If you are captured, the Interplanetary Spy Center will not be able to help you. Only your wits and your sharp Spy skills will help you reach your goals. Be careful. Keep your eyes open at all times.

If you are ready to meet the challenge of being an Interplanetary Spy, turn to page 1.

TOP SECRET

You are cruising through Sector 91 on return from your encounter with the Ultraheroes. Suddenly your ship's scanner picks up a Galactic Danger Alert! You know you are the only Interplanetary Spy in this sector, so you must respond.

To see what the message is, enter your Interplanetary Spy ISBN number below.

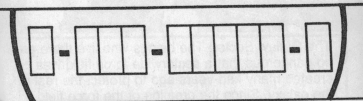

If you are not sure of your number, check the back cover of this book.

Turn to page 2.

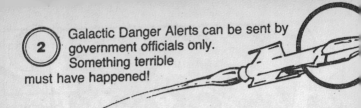

Galactic Danger Alerts can be sent by government officials only. Something terrible must have happened!

You tune in. The message is from Governor Menelon, of Sector 90. It says: "Using a black-hole bomb, three dangerous aliens escaped from Sector 89, the Outlaw Sector. They are now in Sector 90, where they have destroyed fourteen planets in the past few kad-days!"

The Outlaw Sector! The beings who live there are so dangerous that a sectorwide force field was created many kad-years ago to protect the rest of the galaxy. Since the creation of the force field, criminals can enter the Outlaw Sector, but they can't get out.

Go on to the next page.

Governor Menelon's message continues: "The three aliens are known as the Planet Hunters. They destroy planets for sport! Stand by for transmission of a data picture.

3

The Planet Hunters

Venya

Sarvala

Gradak

"The Planet Hunters use a horrible weapon known as the Nethergun. Instead of bullets, the Nethergun fires miniature black holes. Gravitrons inside the Nethergun keep the black holes from destroying the gun and guide the black holes out of the barrel. The gravity fields within even a miniature black hole generate enough power to crush a planet into a lump of matter the size of a marble!"

The Nethergun

Turn to page 4.

The governor continues: "The Planet Hunters' ship is currently docked on the planet Kuzuri, in Sector 90. The ship was damaged during a recent meson dust storm. Kuzuri workers are repairing it under threat of death, but one of them was able to steal blueprints of the ship's design."

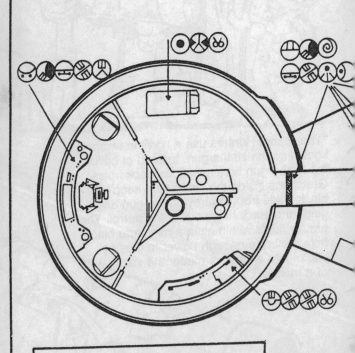

Governor Menelon sends a data picture of the blueprint, and you store it in your wrist scanner.

You notice that the front of the ship is a large living unit, and the back has the chamber containing the rocket engine. A storage section is in the center, between two smaller living units.

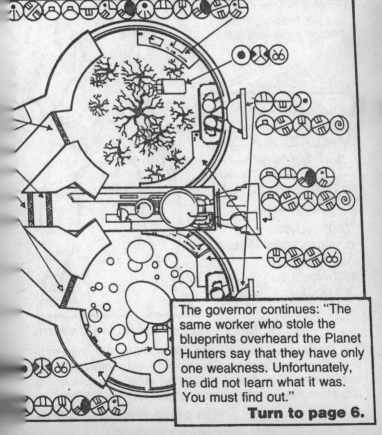

The governor continues: "The same worker who stole the blueprints overheard the Planet Hunters say that they have only one weakness. Unfortunately, he did not learn what it was. You must find out."

Turn to page 6.

The governor's message ends. Quickly you radio Spy Center for clearance. Spy Center sends your orders almost immediately.

Your mission is to go to the planet Kuzuri. There you must get on board the Planet Hunters' ship. Once the ship is in space and away from any inhabited world, you must capture the Planet Hunters before they use the Nethergun to destroy more planets.

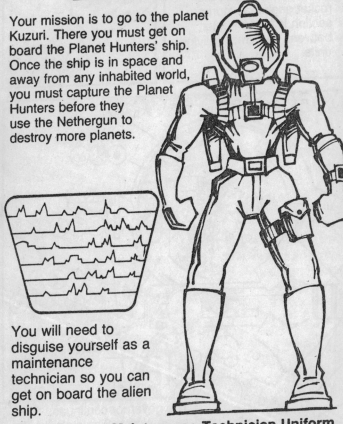

You will need to disguise yourself as a maintenance technician so you can get on board the alien ship.

Maintenance Technician Uniform

Spy Center transmits the specifications for the uniform to your disguise computer. The uniform will protect you from the heat, cold, and vacuum of outer space. It has a rocket backpack with which you can fly short distances.

Go on to the next page.

You will be disguised as a technician in charge of hull cleaning. You will carry a hull-cleaning device that can also function as a powerful weapon. It fires stun rays that are effective against all known living creatures!

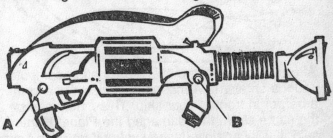

A   **B**

By pressing hidden button A, you can change this device from an ordinary hull cleaner into a stun-ray gun. You fire the gun by pressing button B.

Also, your suit can contain one concealed defensive weapon that can be triggered by a movement of your chin. You must choose whether your suit will fire small metal pellets or whether it will shoot out a small cord with a loop.

Fire metal pellets ☐   **Fire cord with loop** ☐

Record your choice here. Your ship's disguise computer now manufactures your uniform, with the secret defensive weapon you have chosen, and your hull cleaner gun. You put on your uniform.

Turn to page 8.

8 You set your ship's computer for the planet Kuzuri, in Sector 90, and your ship blasts into hyperspace! You are in Sector 91, so it will take you a few kad-hours to get there.

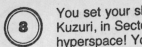

After a short time, the ship's navigation computer sounds an alarm! A meson dust storm has formed a barrier in front of your ship. This must have been the same storm that damaged the Planet Hunters' ship. It will certainly destroy yours if you don't get out of the way fast!

Your ship

Top   Side

In

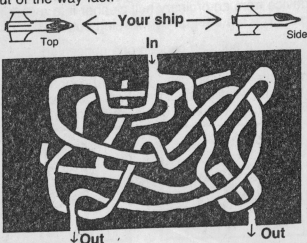

↓Out   ↓Out

In hyperspace, meson dust is so highly charged that it can eat away your ship's hull. Your scanner shows you that there are two paths that you can take through the storm. Which way will lead you to safety without any of the dust touching your ship?

This way?
Turn to page 10.

This way?
Turn to page 13.

You walk down into the spaceport. Before you get very far, you are grabbed by spaceport guard robots.

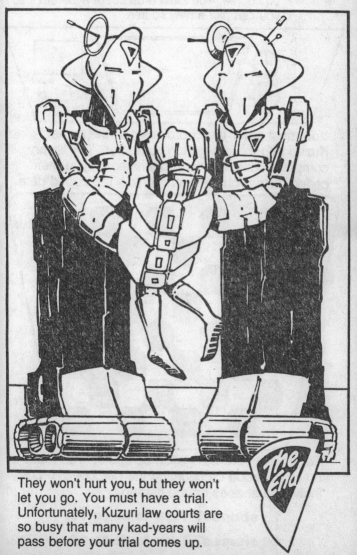

They won't hurt you, but they won't let you go. You must have a trial. Unfortunately, Kuzuri law courts are so busy that many kad-years will pass before your trial comes up.

The End

You avoid the deadly dust of the meson
storm. But your ship's navigation computer
has been damaged by the flight, and you are
off course. You must drop out of hyperdrive so
you can plot a new course.

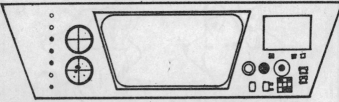

You must enter the coordinates of the planet
Kuzuri into the navigation computer. The library
computer contains the coordinates only in their
coded form. Your screen fills with the coded data.

To program the navigation computer, you must
crack the code by counting the number of
individual shapes on the screen.

13 shapes? Turn to page 15.

14 shapes? Turn to page 12.

Your scanner tells you that the ship is guarded by an automatic protection system. If you try to open any of the closed hatches, you will be blown up.

It is time to see if your disguise works. Casually you walk up to the ship and start cleaning the hull. No one notices you.

You are in luck, Spy! As you clean the rear of the ship, you find a small open hatch. You go inside. The hatch leads to a maze of tubes.

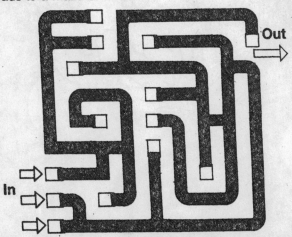

Your scanner tells you that this is a network of fuel tubes. You must get out of here fast because the tubes will soon fill up with fuel. Can you crawl through the tubes quickly enough?

Turn to page 14.

You count fourteen shapes and use that number to program your ship's navigation computer. Then you continue your voyage through hyperspace.

Soon you arrive at the planet Kuzuri.

Turn to page 17.

You try to fly through the deadly meson dust storm.

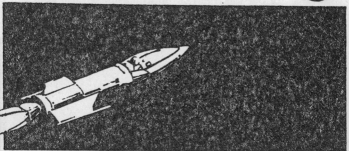

The dust begins to wear away the hull of your ship.

Before you can go back, your ship's hull has been eaten away.

The End

Your suit will be eaten away next, and then you.

You get through the maze of fuel tubes before they are filled. You explore a corridor that runs under the main compartments. On the floor you find a disk with strange writing on it. It seems to be in two languages, only one of which you know.

Can this be a clue about the language of the Planet Hunters? Wait! You hear a noise. You put the disk in your utility pouch and run!

Turn to page 19.

You count thirteen shapes and use that number to reprogram your ship's navigation computer. Then you continue your voyage through hyperspace.

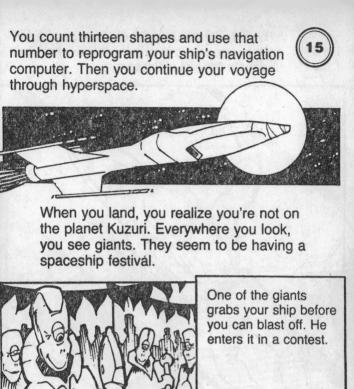

When you land, you realize you're not on the planet Kuzuri. Everywhere you look, you see giants. They seem to be having a spaceship festival.

One of the giants grabs your ship before you can blast off. He enters it in a contest.

Your ship wins first prize! The giant will never let you out of his sight now!

There's only one thing to do. Your hull-cleaner suit has special gravity grips that will hold you tightly to the hull of the ship.

You activate the gravity grips and attach yourself to the hull, just as the Planet Hunters' ship lifts off!

Turn to page 21.

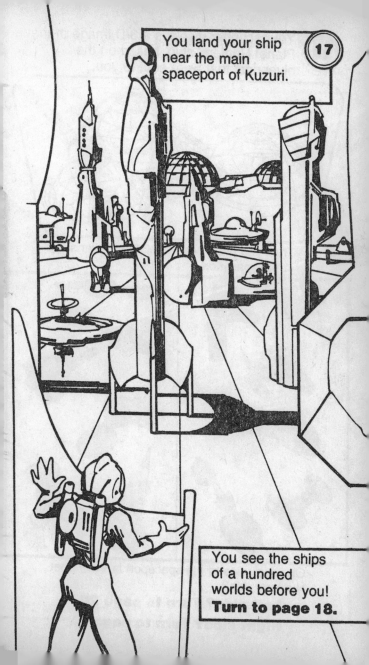

Your scanner displays a 3-D image of the Planet Hunters' ship, based on the blueprints that were sent to you.

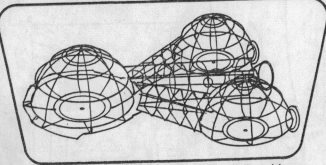

Then you get a scan of all the similar ships in the spaceport.

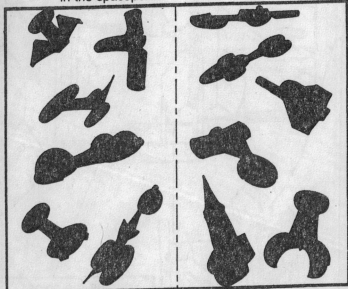

On which side of the spaceport is the Planet Hunters' ship?

Left side? Turn to page 20.

Right side? Turn to page 9.

One of the Planet Hunters is coming! You run through the ship looking for a place to hide.

You're trapped! The only escape is through the hatch you entered earlier. You run through the fuel tubes and jump out of the hatch.

Oh, no! The ship's engines are starting up. If you let the ship get away now, you will have failed your mission.

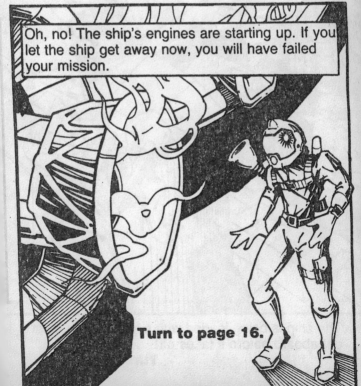

Turn to page 16.

You find the Planet Hunters' ship.
Carefully you creep closer.

The ship is being loaded with supplies. You must
get aboard before it takes off!

Turn to page 11.

You are now in outer space, hanging on to the side of the Planet Hunters' ship. Your uniform protects you.

You look down and see the planet Kuzuri below. Hang on—it's a long way to fall!

Turn to page 22.

Suddenly, the ship's engines stop. This can only mean that the Planet Hunters are preparing to blast into hyperspace. Your gravity grips won't work at hyperspeed—you've got to get inside.

Going hand over hand, you make your way to the back of the ship. The hatch you jumped out of earlier is unlocked. You climb back inside. Since the ship isn't moving, the fuel lines are clear.

Go on to the next page.

You crawl through the fuel tubes until your path is blocked. You go another way. You come to an open space that you analyze with your scanner.

You are inside the rocket engine. The hyperdrive will be starting up in moments. The radiation from the drive will destroy you if you don't get out in time. You must crawl through the engine drive tubes to get out before you're hyper-fried!

Turn to page 24.

Your scanner shows you a picture of the engine drive tubes. You are standing on the left, and you must get to the right.

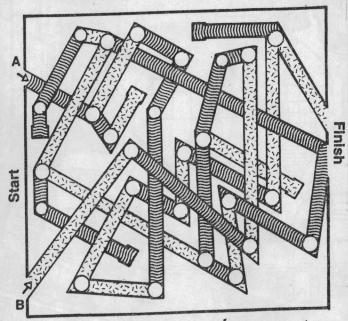

A

Start

B

Finish

These tubes will take you up:

These tubes will take you down: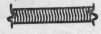

Where should you start?

Tube A? Turn to page 29.

Tube B? Turn to page 26.

Before you can hide, Sarvala, the giant Planet Hunter, comes out of his dome.

He plucks you up like a feather and stuffs you into an interplanetary trash compactor. You'll make a nice paperweight, Spy!

The End

You jump into tube B and go through the tubes, up and down.

You chose the correct tube. You are out of the engine when the main drive starts up. You open an airlock door and look out into the corridor.

There is a closed door in front of you and two corridors that lead to either side. (Check the ship's blueprint on pages 4 and 5.) You are standing in the engine room doorway, so the closed door in front of you leads to Sarvala, the giant. You decide to capture the two smaller Planet Hunters first. Will you take the left corridor or the right?

The left corridor? Turn to page 42.

The right corridor? Turn to page 31.

You cautiously enter Gradak's dome. It looks like a cave. Mushrooms are growing everywhere.

You notice two pictures on the wall. The backgrounds of the pictures are identical. You see Gradak and his family in the first picture, but the second picture is very strange.

You examine the second picture further. Gradak and his family are there, too, but they are disguised! Maybe Gradak has the power to disguise himself as anything he wants.

Turn to page 34.

28

You open a small control panel next to the door. Inside you find the circuits that control the alarm. If you operate the circuits incorrectly, the alarm will go off.

The control panel has several different lights on it. Each light has a unique color and shape. Your scanner analyzes them.

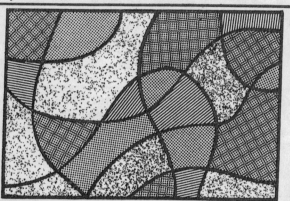

To safely deactivate the alarm, you must turn off the correct lights. Your scanner shows you a master shape. The lights that you want to turn off must black out this master shape:

The buttons below will turn off all the lights of each color. You must choose which two buttons will black out the correct lights to make up the master shape.

Red Blue Green ▨Yellow

If you think turning off the green and yellow lights will black out the master shape, turn to page 25.

If you think turning off the red and blue lights will black out the master shape, turn to page 36.

Hurry, before you are seen!

You start at tube A and ride through the
tubes, going up and down.

29

Unfortunately, your roller coaster ride is still going
on when the engine starts up!

The End

You decide that Gradak is hidden under the picture, disguised as a small footrest. Not taking any chances, you change your hull cleaner into a stun-ray gun and blast the footrest.

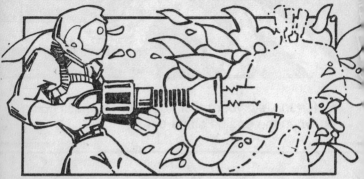

You made a mistake! The "footrest" was a giant ripe puffball! The puffball explodes and covers you with thousands of sticky spores that contain a powerful acid!

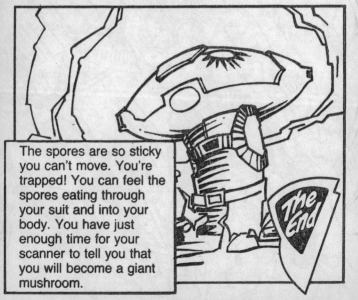

The spores are so sticky you can't move. You're trapped! You can feel the spores eating through your suit and into your body. You have just enough time for your scanner to tell you that you will become a giant mushroom.

You cautiously walk down the right corridor. You come to a double airlock door that has a porthole.

Through the porthole, you see Gradak, the smallest of the Planet Hunters. He shouldn't be too much trouble for you.

Your scanner tells you that the double airlock door has an alarm on it. If you try to open the door, you'll alert the other two Planet Hunters to your presence.

Turn to page 28.

32 The heat instantly rises in the dome. The mushrooms begin to die. "Oh, no, what have you done!" shrieks Gradak. He rushes to save the mushrooms.

You shoot the blaster out of his hand. Then you tie him up. "You've caught me, Spy, but you haven't beaten me yet!" says Gradak with a grin.

Turn to page 43.

You fly through the tunnel safely. You open a hatch and find that you are back in the corridor that led to Gradak's dome.

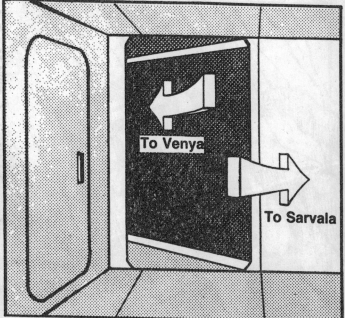

To Venya

To Sarvala

To your far left is the locked airlock that leads to the engine room. In front of you is the corridor that angles left to Venya's dome. The corridor to the right leads to the large dome of the giant.

You must decide which way to go.

If you have already gone to Venya's dome, then you must go right and turn to page 53.

If you haven't gone to Venya's dome yet, go through the corridor in front of you and turn to page 42.

Be sure to examine the blueprint of the ship on pages 4 and 5. It would be unwise to face Sarvala unless you have beaten Venya first.

Carefully you begin to explore the dome.
Gradak must be hidden here somewhere.

You see another picture on the wall.
This one is of all three Planet Hunters.
You see one of their trophies . . . a
planet they have crushed!

Suddenly you realize that Gradak could be anywhere, even right in front of you! He can disguise himself as anything.

Is Gradak hidden under the picture of the three Planet Hunters? Turn to page 30.

Is Gradak hidden under the map of Kranso? Turn to page 39.

You press the buttons that deactivate the alarm. Now you open the airlock. You're ready to fight Gradak.

But when you get inside, Gradak is nowhere to be seen!

Turn to page 27.

You open the control panel and examine the alarm system with your scanner. If you do anything wrong, the control panel's defense system will cause the panel to blow up.

Inside the control panel you see several odd shapes. To deactivate the alarm system, you must remove only the shapes that can completely fill up the square below.

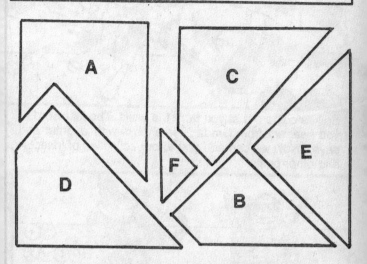

Which shapes will exactly fill up the square?

This is the box that must be filled up exactly with the correct shapes.

Shapes ABC?
Turn to page 46.
Shapes CDE?
Turn to page 45.

38

You start your flight down the tunnel, but you must have picked the wrong flight pattern.

Spikes come out at you from the walls. The last words you hear are from Gradak. He shrieks with laughter and says, "Now we can add you to our collection of insects and other pests!"

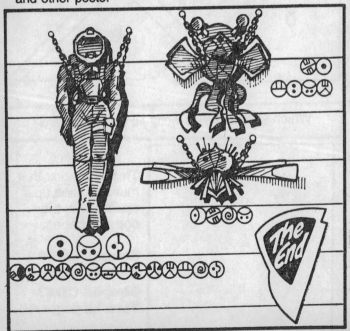

You decide that Gradak is under the map. You press button A on the hull cleaner you are carrying, and it changes into a stun-ray gun. You aim the weapon at the chair. Before you can fire, the chair changes back into Gradak. "Only an Interplanetary Spy could have seen me!" he shouts as he fires his blaster right at you. You quickly dodge out of the way.

"You'll never get me with a hull cleaner!" says Gradak, as he shoots at you again. You fire a stun ray, but Gradak avoids your blast easily. He may be small, but he can bounce around the room faster than you can aim!

Turn to page 58.

Venya whirls around. She seems surprised but not hostile. "You must be one of the hull cleaners. Why didn't you leave the ship before we took off?"

You shrug your shoulders. Venya smiles and says, "I guess we'll just have to drop you off at the next planet."

Then her expression changes. Venya unhooks a strange weapon from her belt. "Better yet, we'll drop you out the airlock now. We have planets to hunt," she adds, laughing cruelly.

Turn to page 49.

You push the wrong buttons!
The lights go out.

41

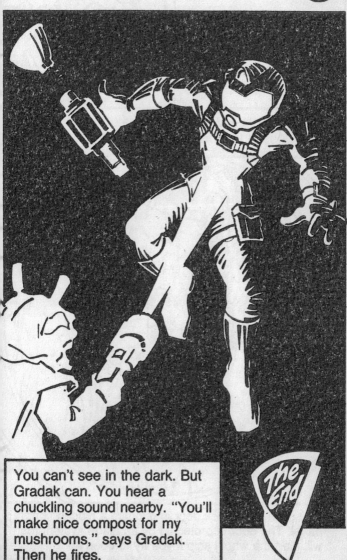

You can't see in the dark. But Gradak can. You hear a chuckling sound nearby. "You'll make nice compost for my mushrooms," says Gradak. Then he fires.

The End

You enter the left corridor and walk until you come to a double airlock door. You peek through a porthole.

Inside you see Venya, the female Planet Hunter. She doesn't look too tough!

You scan the airlock door and locate a hidden control panel. The door is protected by an alarm system that will alert the whole ship if you try to open it.

Turn to page 37.

You suspect that Gradak has probably done something to stop you from leaving the dome. You scan the double airlock door you entered through. During your fight, Gradak locked the door. You can't open it.

While Gradak laughs at you, you explore the dome. Your scanner finds a hidden exit tunnel, and you open the tunnel entrance.

You are about to enter the hidden exit tunnel when your scanner tells you that it's booby-trapped! The top and bottom walls are electrified. Your scanner reports that deadly spikes will shoot out of the circles on the side walls if you break the invisible light beam that goes from each circle to the opposite wall.

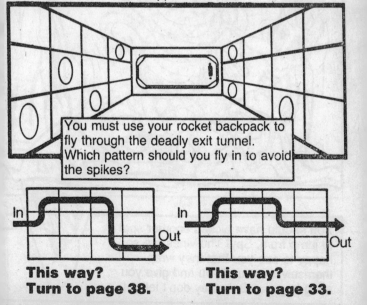

You must use your rocket backpack to fly through the deadly exit tunnel. Which pattern should you fly in to avoid the spikes?

This way? Turn to page 38.

This way? Turn to page 33.

You leap down from the branch.

You should have picked another spot to jump from, Spy! The vines are so happy to see you that they wrap themselves around you and give you a big hug. . . . Only they don't let go!

You deactivate the alarm system and open the door. You enter cautiously, hoping to sneak up on Venya before she turns around.

The dome is like a miniature forest. You try to walk carefully, but you accidentally step on a dry twig!

Turn to page 40.

You made a mistake!

46

The End

The control panel defense system performs its function and blows up in your face. Tough luck, Spy!

The vines are controlled by Venya's singing. You must leap through the vines without letting any of them touch you.

From which position on the branch should you jump down so that you don't hit any vines? You must jump straight down.

Position A?
Turn to page 55.

Position B?
Turn to page 44.

You fire the stun-ray gun and hear a scream from below. Carefully you climb down from the tree to see what has happened.

You have stunned Venya. You take away her weapon and tie her up with dead vines from the dome floor.

Turn to page 61.

Venya fires her weapon. You leap up and grab the overhanging limb of a tree.

"Hold still! I can't blast you without hurting my trees," shouts Venya as you climb higher. The tiny fireballs destroy everything they hit.

Turn to page 52.

You put the cube into the slot. The machine makes strange noises.

You must have put the wrong cube in the slot. The plants are being fed at twice their normal rate! The faster they eat, the hungrier they get! Only an Interplanetary Spy will appeal to them now.

The End

You fire through the leaves on the left side of the dome. The singing stops and you hear Venya say, "So *there* you are!"

51

You have given away your position! Moments later, new plants crawl up the tree and surround you. These look like Spy-eating plants!

The End

You climb higher until you are near the top of the dome. Venya won't be able to see you up here.

Suddenly you hear Venya singing. You look down and see small vines slithering up the tree like snakes! They are coming to get you!

Turn to page 47.

Now you are ready to enter the big dome, inhabited by the giant Planet Hunter, Sarvala.

Wait! Your Spy instinct warns you that something is wrong! Examine the airlock door in front of you carefully. Has anything changed since you last saw it?

If you think something has changed, turn to page 67.

If you don't think anything has changed, turn to page 62.

(Check page 26 if you're not sure.)

Venya wakes up. She looks at you and says, "You aren't really a hull cleaner, are you? You must be some kind of spy! Only an Interplanetary Spy could possibly have gotten this far! But you haven't escaped yet!"

You ignore her because you are busy analyzing the scanner report. The large quantities of potassium in Venya's body puzzle you. Suddenly you hear her moving.

"Spy or not, you should have been smarter than to tie me up with my own vines," says Venya. You thought that the vines were dead, but now they are untying themselves! **Turn to page 57.**

You jump down from the branch and avoid the deadly vines.

You land on a lower branch. From there you grab a vine that doesn't grab you. You swing to a branch high up on another tree.

Venya is still singing! If you don't figure out a way to stop her, the next plants you encounter may get you.

Turn to page 70.

You leave Venya safely tied up and go through an airlock. You are in the same corridor that you were in before you went into Venya's dome.

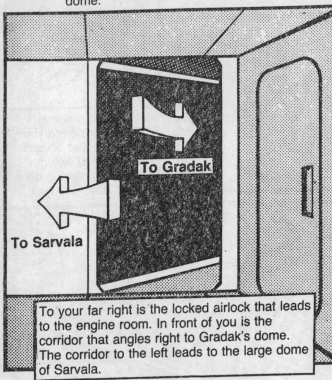

To Gradak

To Sarvala

To your far right is the locked airlock that leads to the engine room. In front of you is the corridor that angles right to Gradak's dome. The corridor to the left leads to the large dome of Sarvala.

You must decide which way to go.

If you have already gone to Gradak's dome, then go left and turn to page 53.

If you haven't gone to Gradak's dome yet, then go through the corridor in front of you and turn to page 31.

Be sure to examine the blueprint of the ship on pages 4 and 5. It would be unwise to face Sarvala unless you have beaten Gradak first.

Venya is free again. As long as she can use her plants against you, you won't be able to beat her.

57

You see a machine that Venya uses to feed her plants continually. These plants need large amounts of a special plant food to be able to move around as fast as they do.

You scanner tells you that you can stop the plant food machine by putting the correct control cube in the slot.

If the correct control cube were unfolded, this is what it would look like:

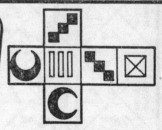

A

B

Which of these cubes is the correct cube?

Cube A? Turn to page 50.
Cube B? Turn to page 65.

58 You've got to find some way to stop Gradak before one of his blasts hits you. You see an environmental-control panel nearby. Quickly, in between dodging blasts, you use your scanner to see how it works.

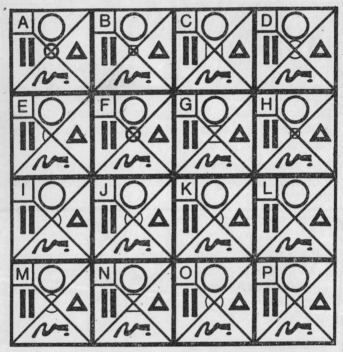

If you can push the two buttons that do not match any other button, you can raise the temperature inside the dome, which will cause Gradak's mushrooms to die. The mushrooms are Gradak's only food.

Push buttons J and M? Turn to page 41.
Push buttons E and L? Turn to page 32.

Suddenly the dome bursts open. Sarvala breaks through the glass. He aims the Nethergun at you!

Turn to page 86.

Frantically you try to repair your rocket backpack. You succeed! But there is enough fuel left for only one burst.

You see a slowly moving meteor coming toward you. If you can grab onto it, it will take you in the direction of the ship.

You grab onto the meteor and ride it. Suddenly your scanner goes on alert. It shows you that a meteor swarm is moving across the path of the meteor you are riding. A collision would be deadly!

Your scanner gives you more bad news. A very fast meteor is going to strike the meteor you're riding in a matter of moments!

Turn to page 77.

You are curious about the body chemistry of a Planet Hunter. You scan Venya's body. Maybe you can get a clue to her secret weakness.

Your scanner reports that Venya's body chemistry is different from that of most humans or humanoids.

		Human	Venya
Potassium			
Lithium-Sulphur-Lithium			
Hydrogen-Oxygen-Hydrogen			

You find high levels of lithium and sulphur, where you might expect to find hydrogen and oxygen. You also find high levels of potassium.

Turn to page 54.

You decide that the airlock looks the same as it did before. You're ready to face the last of the three Planet Hunters.

You open the door. An ultrasonic blast knocks you down! The giant Planet Hunter must have thought you were an interplanetary traveling salesman!

The End

You try to activate your rocket backpack, but the giant damaged it when he grabbed you.

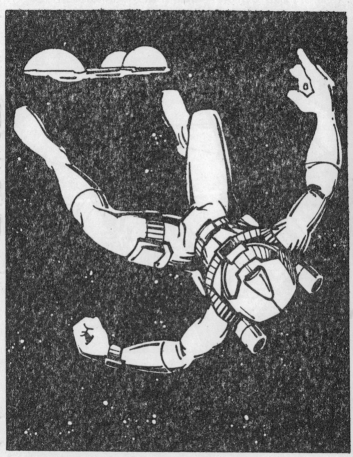

You look in the direction of the Planet Hunters' spaceship. You're floating away from it, getting farther away every moment. You will be lost in space!

Turn to page 60.

The hatch leads to the outside of the ship! Because you were wearing your suit, you didn't even realize that the inner corridor was open to outer space.

Your best bet is to sneak up on Sarvala from the outside. Carefully you crawl along the hull and make your way to the forward dome.

Turn to page 59.

You put the cube into the slot. The machine stops! Now the plants can't move fast enough to attack you.

You grab Venya before she can escape. "You won't get away with this, you rotten Spy!" she says as you tie her up with her own rope. "You may have captured me, but I'm not the only Planet Hunter on this ship."

Turn to page 56.

You fire your rocket backpack. The meteor you're riding changes direction, but it doesn't get out of the way of the approaching meteor.

The collision sends you spinning into the densest part of the meteor swarm.

The End

You examine the door carefully. The sign
on it has changed!

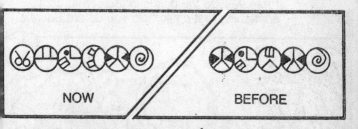

NOW

BEFORE

You'd better try to get in some other way.

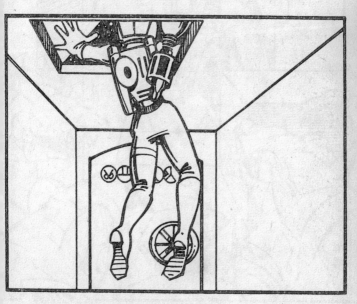

You look upward and see an open hatch. You
boost yourself up.

Turn to page 64.

You decide that the writing says DO NOT ENTER. Since you can't figure out how to get inside the tank, you examine the rest of the room. Maybe the boxes in the corner contain something that could help you defeat Sarvala.

You move a box and see a hole in the metal wall behind it. You hear a screeching noise and jump back. Giant mutant metallic rats come out of the hole. You've seen rats on ships before, but never rats like these!

The End

You push the wrong sequence! The hatch blows up, and the blast sends you back into space.

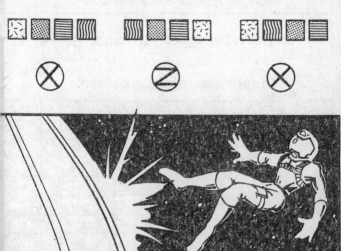

You can see the Planet Hunters' ship jumping into hyperspace. They're going to leave you behind! Now you are lost in space . . . forever.

You scan the whole dome below you. If you can find Venya in the scan picture, you might be able to knock her out.

This is the symbol for Venya:

This is a scan of the whole dome:

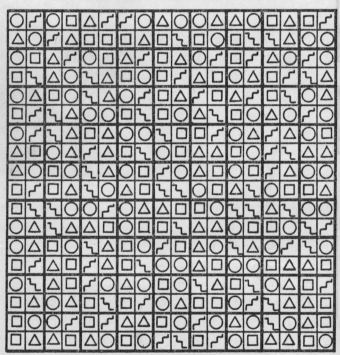

Where is Venya?

On the left?   **On the right?**
Turn to page 51.   **Turn to page 48.**

Hurry, before a new plant menace strikes.

Maybe you can figure out what the writing on the tank says. The disk you picked up earlier had writing on it. (If you don't remember what the disk looks like, turn to page 14.)

(If you don't remember what the disk looks like, turn to page 14.)

You look at the writing on the disk:

You look at the writing on the tank:

Your scanner indicates that these letters go with these symbols:

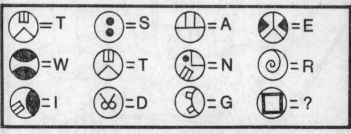

Can you tell what the tank says?

If you think it says DANGER WATER, turn to page 75.

If you think it says DO NOT ENTER, turn to page 68.

If you think it says DANGER WATER, turn to page 75.

If you think it says DO NOT ENTER, turn to page 68.

The giant pushes Venya and Gradak away. "We're going to keep the Spy until we find out why he's here," he says. Then he ties you to a huge control couch.

You hear the Planet Hunters talking. They are discussing two nearby planets. "Which one do you want to destroy, Venya? It's your turn to pick," Sarvala says.

Turn to page 85.

You fire your rocket backpack and cling to your meteor as it changes direction. You fly through space!

You miss all the meteors! You had one chance in a million and you made it, Spy!

You scan ahead and see that your luck is holding out. You are heading right for the Planet Hunters' ship.

Turn to page 76.

74 The giant grabs you.

Sarvala's grip is so strong that it begins to crush the rocket pack on your back.

Without warning, he throws you into space!

Turn to page 63.

You decide that the writing on the tank says DANGER WATER. Why would the Planet Hunters think that water was dangerous?

Using your scanner, you analyze more of the letters of the Planet Hunters' alphabet on the boxes around you. Your scanner displays their complete alphabet:

Turn to page 100.

76

Getting *into* the Planet Hunters' ship will be harder than getting *out*! When you entered before, the hatch was wide open, but now it's locked. You study the two buttons and four lights on the control panel for the hatch lock.

 Pushing this button causes the lights to change in the following manner:

Start   **First Push**   **Second Push**

 Pushing this button causes the lights to change in the following manner:

Start   **First Push**   **Second Push**

The panel lights look like this now:

Your scanner tells you that if you can get the panel lights to look like this:

you can open the hatch safely. A button can be pushed more than once. What sequence of button pushes will work?

This sequence of button pushes? Turn to page 69.

This sequence of button pushes? Turn to page 80.

You must change the direction of the
meteor you're riding on. There's just one
burst of fuel left in your rocket backpack,
and you've got to make it count.

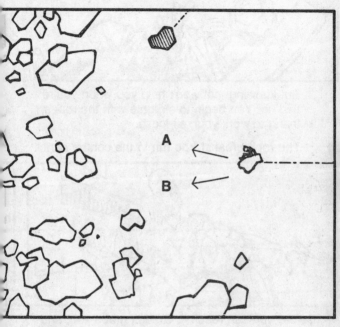

 APPROACHING METEOR

 YOUR METEOR

In which direction do you want to move?

Direction A? Turn to page 66.

Direction B? Turn to page 73.

78

You decide that the sign says
DROP WHEEL, which must refer
to the landing wheels of the ship.

But knowing that won't help you when you're
tied up. You begin to struggle with the ropes,
trying to work yourself loose.

The rope breaks! You run to the control panel.

Before you can reach it, Gradak grabs you, and
Venya will back him up!

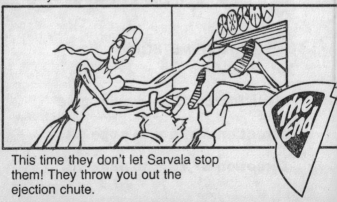

This time they don't let Sarvala stop
them! They throw you out the
ejection chute.

Before you can do anything, Sarvala grabs you and pulls you out of the hatch. He takes away your weapon.

"I see you came back for more," says the grinning giant. "My partners will be most happy to see you." He takes you into the forward control room.

There you see Gradak and Venya.

"Let me at that Interplanetary Spy!" says Gradak.

"No chance," says Venya, pushing the short Planet Hunter out of the way. "I have my revenge all planned out."

Turn to page 72.

You push the buttons in the correct sequence, and the hatch opens.

You enter one of the ship's storerooms, looking for some way to defeat the giant. You see a large tank in front of you, with writing on it.

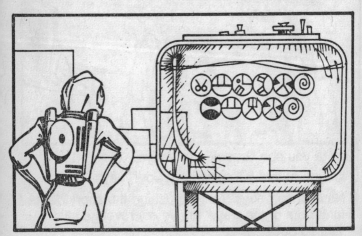

Turn to page 71.

Forty-three kad-seconds isn't a long time.
You can't let him get a second shot. You
fire at Sarvala with your stun-ray gun.

The blast bounces off him harmlessly! The other
Planet Hunters weren't as tough as this one.
Through the intercom, you hear Sarvala laughing.
Then he shouts, "I don't need to waste the
Nethergun on a puny human!"

He reaches out to grab you!

Turn to page 74.

With a movement of your chin, you eject the cord with the loop on the end of it. It shoots into the air, but it *misses* the button you were trying to hit.

Gradak runs over. He grabs the end of the cord before you can pull it back. "You just don't give up, do you?" he says as he pulls on the loop.

Thinking fast, you operate a mechanism that cuts the cord from inside your suit. Gradak pulls so hard that he crashes back against the control panel.

The panel bursts into flames behind him!

Turn to page 90.

You dive forward and stop Gradak from pulling rope B.

Unfortunately, Gradak pulls rope A. He leaps aside just as all the rocks and logs fall down on you!

You find it a crushing experience!

As the ship gets close to the surface of the water planet, the Planet Hunters bail out in safety pods.

You ride the ship down into the water.

You are not hurt. You climb out and see that there are several islands nearby. Each of the Planet Hunters lands on a different one.

You swim toward one of the islands.

Turn to page 93.

You scan the control panel of the ship. Is there anything you can do to stop the Planet Hunters before they destroy another planet?

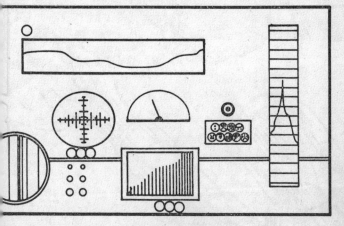

You see a button with a sign under it. Could that be a danger signal? Here's what the sign says:

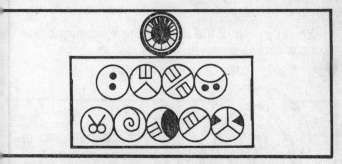

Do you think it says DROP WHEEL? If so, turn to page 78.

Do you think it says STOP DRIVE? If so, turn to page 89.

(If you're not sure, check the alphabet on page 75.)

You dive out of the way as the miniature black hole zooms past you and is lost in space.

Your scanner picks up Sarvala's space intercom. You hear him mutter, "Blast! The gun will take forty-three kad-seconds to recharge."

Turn to page 81.

With a movement of your chin, you fire a metal pellet from inside your suit. It's hard to aim when you're tied down. You miss!

Venya hears the firing sound. She comes at you with her weapon drawn. "I'm going to make sure you never do that again!" she says as she raises her weapon.

You fire another one of the metal pellets at Venya. It causes her own shot to go wild. Venya's blast hits the control panel!

Turn to page 90.

You climb to the top of the cliff.

But Gradak is nowhere in sight! You must find him.
There are many animal tracks in the muddy ground.

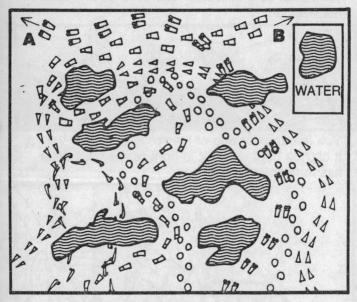

In which direction did Gradak go?

Direction A? Turn to page 111.

Direction B? Turn to page 92.

The sign says STOP DRIVE. If the "drive" is the ship's stardrive, then the ship won't be able to move if you stop it. But how can you get to the button? If you struggle, one of the Planet Hunters will notice and stop you.

You suddenly remember that your suit has a built-in defensive device. Which one did you choose? (Check page 7, if you don't remember.) Can you use the device to hit the button without leaving the couch?

Fire metal pellets

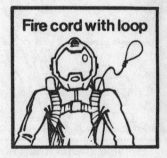

Fire cord with loop

If you chose the device that fires metal pellets, turn to page 87.

If you chose the device that fires a cord with a loop, turn to page 82.

90

"What did you let that Spy do?" shouts Sarvala angrily. "The control panel is on fire!"

"The stardrive has stopped!" wails Gradak.

"We must start it again quickly, or we'll crash," screams Venya.

Sarvala calms them down and says, "We'll go to the engine room and see if we can restart the stardrive there." All three Planet Hunters rush to the engine room, leaving you alone.

Go on to the next page.

The Planet Hunters' ship is almost out of control! Using your Spy strength, you break free of the ropes.

Your scanner analyzes the damage. The ship will crash soon. You see two planets. One is a desert world and the other is a water world. The ship must smash into one of them.

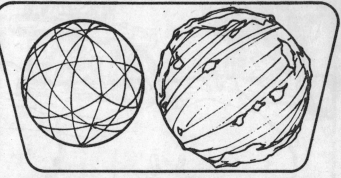

Think carefully, Spy! You must guide the falling ship to the planet where it will be easiest for you to capture the Planet Hunters.

The desert planet? Turn to page 96.

The water planet? Turn to page 101.

(If you need a hint, look at pages 35, 61, and 71.)

You realize that Gradak's tracks wouldn't go through any of the pools of water. You find him and see that he has built a trap. "You try anything and I'll pull one of these ropes," Gradak says. Pulling on the ropes will make the structures collapse, but only one of the structures will collapse completely. If that happens, you'll be crushed!

You must stop Gradak from pulling the rope that will cause a complete collapse. Which one must he *not* pull?

Rope A? Turn to page 104.

Rope B? Turn to page 83.

"I may not be strong," jeers Gradak. "But I can build a good trap!"

You swim to the island with high cliffs. Once you are on the shore, you begin looking for whichever Planet Hunter landed here.

"You'll never get me!" someone shouts. You look up and see Gradak at the top of the cliffs!

Can you climb all the way up the steep cliff without falling?

Turn to page 120.

You start out through the jungle. At first you are able to safely move from one plant to another.

Then you make a mistake. The plants don't like your version of hopscotch!

You tell her that you will leave her here for now, but you will return when you have captured Sarvala. **Turn to page 110.**

You set the controls for the desert planet. You strap yourself in and prepare for a rough landing.

You and the Planet Hunters are found by desert nomads.

The nomads offer to help the Planet Hunters—if they can have *you* for a present.

The End

One of the nomads' robo-camels is broken. You are the replacement!

You climb up and down the ledges and tunnels, but you don't seem to be getting any closer to the top.

You are getting tired. Suddenly your foot slips. It's a looooooong waaaaaaaay dooooooooown!

The scanner tells you that the plants in the jungle are hostile to all animal and human life. But if you move in a certain way, you can avoid being hurt.

In ➡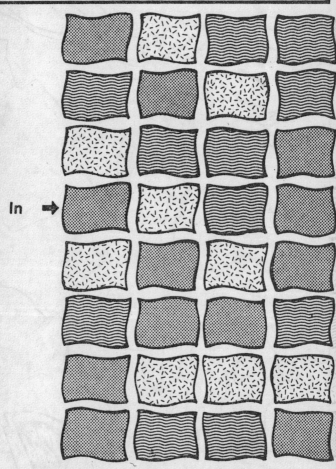

The plants will allow you to live only if you move from *one kind* of plant to *another kind*.

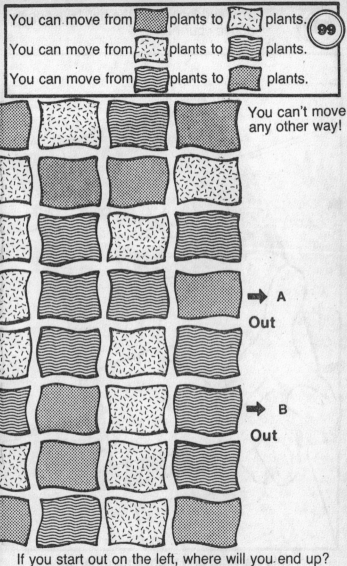

You can move from ▦ plants to ⬚ plants.

You can move from ⬚ plants to 〰 plants.

You can move from 〰 plants to ▦ plants.

99

You can't move
any other way!

➡ A

Out

➡ B

Out

If you start out on the left, where will you end up?

Exit A? Turn to page 103.

Exit B? Turn to page 94.

You suddenly hear the hatchway open above your head.

It is Sarvala, and there's no other way out of the room!

Turn to page 79.

You set the controls for the water planet. Your Spy intuition has put together several facts:

There were no rivers, lakes, or oceans shown on the map of the Planet Hunters' home. (If you don't remember, check page 35.)

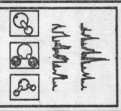

Also, there is no water in the bodies of the Planet Hunters. Instead of water (hydrogen and oxygen), their bodies have lithium and sulphur. (If you don't remember, check page 61.)

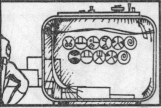

Finally, you found a tank of water labeled DANGER WATER. (If you don't remember, check page 71.)

If water is dangerous to the Planet Hunters, then the water planet is where you want to go! You set the controls to take the ship there.

Turn to page 84.

102 Before she wakes up, you tie Venya with vines. Using your scanner, you make sure that these vines won't respond to her powers.

"What . . . happened?" says Venya. "I feel faint."

You ask her if she would like some water.

Turn to page 95.

You make it through the deadly jungle safely. You scan in all four directions to see if you can find any Planet Hunters.

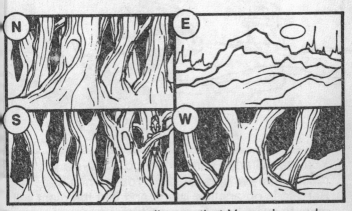

Stop! Your scanner tells you that Venya is nearby.

You scan in all four directions again.

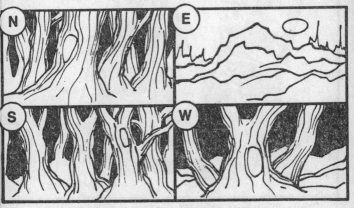

Which way did Venya go?

North? Turn to page 106.
South? Turn to page 113.

You stop Gradak from pulling rope A, but he pulls the one on the right. The trap doesn't collapse completely!

You grab Gradak and tie him up. "Sarvala will rescue me!" whines Gradak. You tell him that Sarvala is on another island and that the giant will have to swim here to rescue him.

"Swim!" shouts Gradak. "He can't do that! I'm doomed!" You reassure Gradak that Spy Center will take care of him.

Go on to the next page.

You leave Gradak behind and swim to the next island. You don't know which of the two other Planet Hunters you'll find, but you can't rest until all three are captured.

When you reach the island you find it is covered with thick jungle.

You'll need your scanner to tell you what is ahead.

Turn to page 98.

The End

You turn around and see eyes. Hundreds of eyes! The plants here have eyes . . . and teeth . . . and claws!

The natives approach.

You ask them if they have seen any giants.

Turn to page 114.

The trees in this part of the forest are so tall that you can't see Sarvala.

Using your scanner, you find a path through the maze of forest trees that will lead you to Sarvala.

In

Out

Follow the path to page 115.

You remember that Sarvala's body contains extremely large amounts of potassium. You know that potassium will burn if it touches water. Looking around, you see a puddle of water nearby. You splash the water toward Sarvala.

Sarvala looks worried and steps back. You splash him again, closer this time. You tell him that if he doesn't surrender, you'll splash him all over. "Oh, no!" says Sarvala, falling back. "How did you ever find out that water can burn us?" Then he surrenders.

Turn to page 116.

You can see a village near the shore. Maybe the inhabitants can help you against Sarvala.

Turn to page 107.

You follow the tracks through the muddy ground. Suddenly you find out what made the tracks. It isn't Gradak!

The End

You don't know what kind of animal this is. All you know is that it has the biggest teeth you've ever seen . . . or ever *will* see.

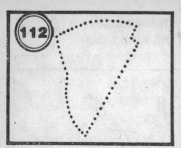

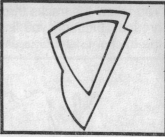

You see a familiar dot pattern on one of the towers in the village.

It is the Interplanetary Spy symbol!

Quickly you show them your Interplanetary Spy identification card.

They know that you are the one to trust! Their chief speaks: "Long ago an Interplanetary Spy visited us and told us to trust all those that carry the identification card."

Turn to page 117.

You go south, creeping cautiously through the jungle.

You see Venya ahead of you. Quickly you climb up a tree.

You drop down on her and knock her out!

Turn to page 102.

The natives step aside. Sarvala walks out of one of their huts! He is their friend! What can you do now?

You must act quickly before the natives capture you. You look around the village.

If you see something that might help you, turn to page 112.

If you don't see anything that could help you, turn to page 119.

You make your way through
the maze of trees.

Sarvala is waiting for you on the other side. "Take
one more step, Spy, and I'll blast you with the
Nethergun!" **Turn to page 118.**

Now that you have captured the last of the three Planet Hunters, you program your scanner to send an emergency radio message, requesting assistance.

You retrieve the Nethergun and hide it until a ship arrives.

The natives help you get the other two Planet Hunters safely to their island. Soon you see a large starship hovering overhead. The face in the pilot's window looks familiar. **Turn to page 121.**

You ask the natives to help you capture Sarvala. They surround him.

He laughs and easily knocks them out of his way. "I didn't like the food here anyway!" he says as he strolls away into the forest.

You follow him. As long as he has the Nethergun, he can destroy planets! **Turn to page 108.**

118 Sarvala is bluffing. You know that if he fires the Nethergun at you, the black hole from the Nethergun will destroy the entire planet, including Sarvala himself. You leap forward and kick the Nethergun out of his hands.

Growling, Sarvala says, "I don't need it anyway. I can destroy you with my bare hands!"

Turn to page 109.

The natives, however, will be
most helpful . . . to Sarvala!

Your scanner shows you that there are several ledges and tunnels you can use to get to the top of the cliff.

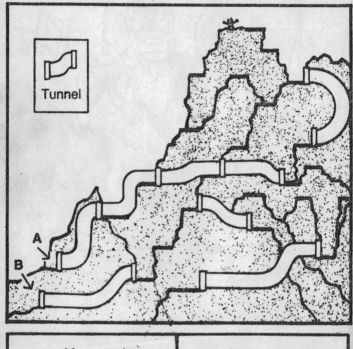

Tunnel

You can jump up to a ledge only if it is no higher than this:

You can jump down to a ledge only if it is no lower than this:

You can crawl up or down any tunnel. Which tunnel should you start out in?

Tunnel A? Turn to page 88.

Tunnel B? Turn to page 97.

The pilot is Prince Quizon, from the planet Alvare! "I was cruising nearby and heard your message," the prince says. "I'll help you take these criminals to Spy Center."

Congratulations, Spy! You captured the three deadly Planet Hunters before they could use the fearsome Nethergun again. Not only that, but you have discovered that water is the Planet Hunters' secret weakness. They will never threaten the galaxy again, and Spy Center will dismantle the Nethergun once and for all!

The End

We hope you enjoyed reading this book. All the titles currently available in the Interplanetary Spy series are listed on page two. Ask for them in your local bookshop or local paperback stockist.

If you would like to know more about these books, or if you have difficulty obtaining any of them locally, or if you would like to tell us what you think of the series, write to: —

Interplanetary Spy,
Corgi Books,
Century House,
61–63 Uxbridge Road,
London W5 5SA.